W9-BEM-105

Dedicated to anybody who ever made a mistake
—D. G.

Dedicated to the home team—Christy, Noah, Lilah, and Blue
—K. T.

Text copyright © 2011 by Dan Gutman
Illustrations copyright © 2011 by Kerry Talbott
All rights reserved. No part of this book may be reproduced or transmitted in any form or by any means,
electronic or mechanical, including photocopying, recording, or by any information storage and
retrieval system, without permission in writing from the publisher.

First published in the United States of America in October 2011
by Bloomsbury Books for Young Readers
www.bloomsburykids.com

For information about permission to reproduce selections from this book, write to
Permissions, Bloomsbury BFYR, 175 Fifth Avenue, New York, New York 10010

Library of Congress Cataloging-in-Publication Data
Gutman, Dan.
The day Roy Riegels ran the wrong way / by Dan Gutman ; illustrated by Kerry Talbott. — 1st U.S. ed.
       p.   cm.
Summary: A boy's grandfather tells him about the famous Rose Bowl game in 1929 when the University
of California Golden Bears lost after one of their players ran the wrong way down the football field.
ISBN 978-1-59990-494-8 (hardcover) • ISBN 978-1-59990-495-5 (reinforced)
1. Riegels, Roy—Juvenile fiction. [1. Riegels, Roy—Fiction. 2. Football—History—Fiction.
3. Grandfathers—Fiction.] I. Talbott, Kerry, ill. II. Title.
PZ7.G9846Day 2011   [E]—dc22   2010043098

Art created with mixed/digital media
Typeset in Bodoni Six
Book design by John Candell

Printed in China by C&C Offset Printing Co., Ltd., Shenzhen, Guangdong
2 4 6 8 10 9 7 5 3 1 (hardcover)
2 4 6 8 10 9 7 5 3 1 (reinforced)

All papers used by Bloomsbury Publishing, Inc., are natural, recyclable products
made from wood grown in well-managed forests. The manufacturing processes
conform to the environmental regulations of the country of origin.

THE DAY ROY RIEGELS RAN THE WRONG WAY

Dan Gutman

illustrated by Kerry Talbott

BLOOMSBURY

NEW YORK BERLIN LONDON SYDNEY

Did I ever tell you about a football player named Roy Riegels?
Not another one of your stories from the dark ages, Grandpa!

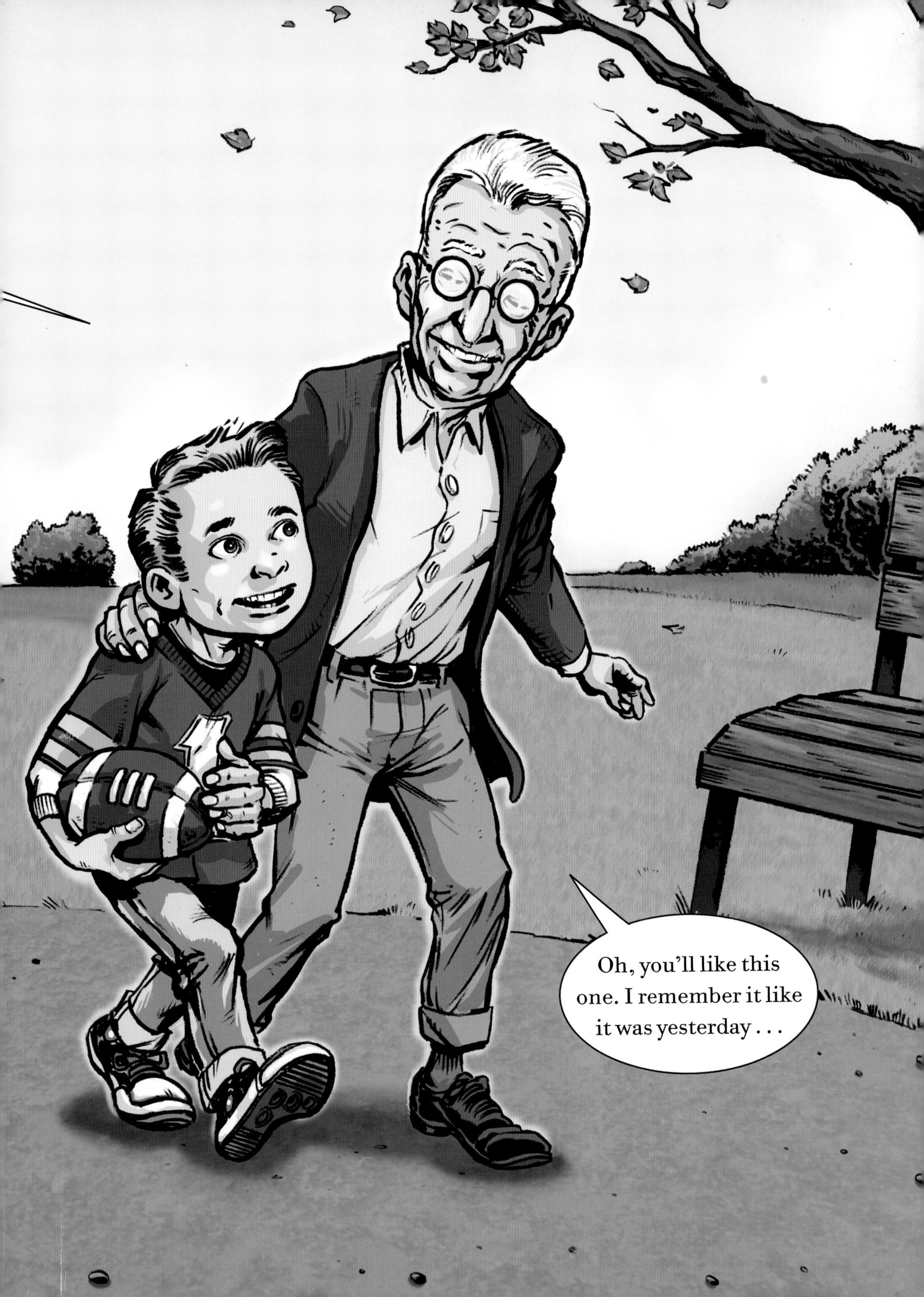
Oh, you'll like this one. I remember it like it was yesterday . . .

Here comes the home team, the Golden Bears. The giants of the gridiron. The monsters of the midway. The guardians of the goal line. First on the field is their center, Roy Riegels.
Let's make some history today, fellows.
You bet, Roy.
Did Roy Riegels score a famous touchdown, Grandpa?
Nope.

Oh, it's a battle out there, folks. At the end of the first quarter, neither team has scored.

The Golden Bears drove all the way down to the Georgia Tech 25-yard line before giving up the ball. There are just a few minutes left in the first half, ladies and gentlemen. Stumpy Thomason of Georgia Tech takes the snap and swings wide left. He has some blockers.

But, oh, wait! A gang of Bears comes out of nowhere and flattens him!

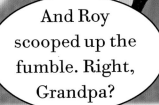

And Roy scooped up the fumble. Right, Grandpa?

You'll see.

The pigskin is loose! It's anybody's ball! It looks like Roy Riegels of the Golden Bears is going to grab it!

This should be interesting. Roy is the center. I don't know if he's ever run with the ball, folks.

Well, he's running today.
Riegels takes two steps
toward the sideline!
He bounces off one tackler.

He spins away from another.
Riegels sees running room!

Roy is tearing down the sideline like a scared deer!
Nobody is close to him! It looks like he's going to score
a touchdown! But there's just one problem . . .

What am I seeing? Am I crazy? Riegels is past midfield! He's at the 40-yard line! The 30! But he's running the wrong direction!

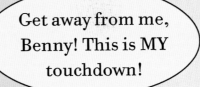

Wait a minute! Riegels has stopped at the 1-yard line!
It looks like he realizes he ran the wrong way!

But it's too late to turn around! Georgia Tech wrestles him to the ground right there!

Yup. But they decided to punt instead.

So now California has to go back 99 yards, Grandpa?

Cal has to punt from their own end zone. But here comes Georgia Tech's Vance Maree diving for the ball! He got a hand on it! The ball bounces free! It's rolling out of bounds! That will be a safety!

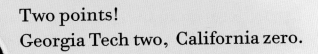

Two points!
Georgia Tech two, California zero.

I ruined everything, Coach. I ruined my school. I ruined myself. I can't go out there again. I couldn't face that crowd to save my life.

What's done is done, Roy. You can't erase that mistake. But it's in the past. Now get up and go back out there. This game is only half over.

What happened after that, Grandpa? Did Roy go back out there?
Yup, and he played a great second half too. He even blocked a punt. It just goes to show that mistakes are not the end of the world. It's what you do after the mistake that counts.
Did YOU ever make a mistake like that, Grandpa?
A million of 'em. But I will say this— I never made the same one twice.

• A NOTE FROM THE AUTHOR •

This is a true story. The California Golden Bears lost that game 8–7, and Roy Riegels's wrong-way run became one of the most famous moments in football history. But Roy didn't let it get him down. He became the captain of the team the next year. After college, he was a high school football coach. He served in the army during World War II. When the war was over, he started his own fertilizer company. Roy was elected to the University of California Athletic Hall of Fame and the Rose Bowl Hall of Fame.

After a while, Roy was able to laugh about his famous wrong-way run. He even performed it in theaters for people to enjoy. He lived to be eighty-four years old—and for the rest of his life, people called him "Wrong-Way Riegels."